KATIE WOO and PEDRO Mysteries

The Mystery of the Snow Puppy

by Fran Manushkin

illustrated by Tammie Lyon

PICTURE WINDOW BOOKS

a capstone imprint

Published by Picture Window Books, an imprint of Capstone
1710 Roe Crest Drive, North Mankato, Minnesota 56003
capstonepub.com

Text copyright © 2022 by Fran Manushkin
Illustrations copyright © 2022 by Capstone

Library of Congress Cataloging-in-Publication Data
Names: Manushkin, Fran, author. | Lyon, Tammie, illustrator.
Title: The mystery of the snow puppy / by Fran Manushkin; illustrated by
Tammie Lyon.
Description: North Mankato, Minnesota : Picture Window Books, an imprint
of Capstone, [2022] | Series: Katie and Pedro mysteries | Audience: Ages 5-7.
| Audience: Grades K-1. | Summary: When Koko, Katie's new white puppy,
is scared by a noisy truck and runs away, Katie and Pedro try to track her
down in the snow, following several false leads until they finally see Koko.
Identifiers: LCCN 2021016012 (print) | LCCN 2021016013 (ebook) | ISBN
9781663958655 (hardcover) | ISBN 9781666332100 (paperback) | ISBN
9781666332117 (pdf)
Subjects: LCSH: Woo, Katie (Fictitious character)—Juvenile fiction. |
Chinese Americans—Juvenile fiction. | Hispanic Americans—Juvenile fiction.
| Dogs—Juvenile fiction. | Detective and mystery stories. | CYAC: Mystery
and detective stories. | Dogs—Fiction. | Lost and found possessions—Fiction.
| Chinese Americans—Fiction. | Hispanic Americans—Fiction. | LCGFT:
Detective and mystery fiction.
Classification: LCC PZ7.M3195 My 2022 (print) | LCC PZ7.M3195 (ebook) |
DDC 813.54 [E]—dc23
LC record available at https://lccn.loc.gov/2021016012
LC ebook record available at https://lccn.loc.gov/2021016013

Design Elements by Shutterstock: Darcraft, Magnia
Designed by Dina Her

Table of Contents

Chapter 1

Katie's New Puppy

Katie has a new puppy.

Her name is Koko.

Koko is white as snow.

Her tail looks like a long

feather!

Koko loves burgers.

When Katie's mom calls,

"Burgers for supper," Koko

comes running.

One snowy day, Katie and
Pedro were playing with Koko
in the yard.

Suddenly a big noisy truck
came by and scared Koko.

"Arf!" She barked and ran
away.

"Stop!" yelled Katie and Pedro. But Koko didn't stop. Koko kept running. She ran around the corner and was gone!

Chapter 2

Collecting Clues

"Let's look for her tracks," said Katie. "That will be a clue. If we follow them, we will find Koko!"

Katie and
Pedro began
looking.

"I see some
tracks!" yelled
Pedro.

"Those are
cat tracks," said
Katie. "That is
not Koko."

"I see squirrel tracks,"

said Pedro.

"And rabbit tracks," said

Katie. "But no Koko."

Pedro pointed to a snowy hill. "I see dog tracks! That is the clue we are looking for."

They began running up the big hill.

"I see a white dog," said

Pedro. "It must be Koko!"

"No!" said Katie.

"Someone made a puppy

out of snow."

"Let's look for a long white tail," said Katie. "That is a clue to lead us to Koko."

"I see one!" yelled Pedro.

They ran after it.

"Oh no!" said Katie.

"That's not my puppy. It's a

feather on a lady's hat."

"Don't give up!" said
Pedro.

"Look!" said Katie. "A
white dog is rolling down
the hill."

Was it Koko?

No! It was a boy in a

white snowsuit.

Chapter 3

Finding Koko

Katie told Pedro, "We need more clues. Koko likes to ride on my scooter. Maybe she jumped on a sled."

Katie yelled, "I see something white riding on that sled."

Was it Koko?

"Yes!" yelled Katie. "It's
Koko. She is wagging her
tail. She looks very happy!"

Her sled was zooming
fast, fast, FAST!

She was heading for a

big tree!

"Koko!" yelled Katie.

"Jump off! Koko, come!"

But Koko didn't come. She stayed on the sled. The tree was getting closer and closer.

Katie yelled, "BURGERS FOR SUPPER!"

AAAARFFF!

Koko jumped off the sled

and ran to Katie. Koko was

safe! Katie hugged Koko over

and over.

"Yay!" shouted Pedro.

"We solved the mystery of

the missing puppy!"

That night, they had a
big happy dinner. Can you
guess what they ate?

About the Author

Fran Manushkin is the author of Katie Woo, the highly acclaimed fan-favorite early-reader series, as well as the popular Pedro series. Her other books include *Happy in Our Skin*, *Plenty of Hugs!*, *Baby, Come Out!*, and the best-selling board books *Big Girl Panties* and *Big Boy Underpants*. There is a real Katie Woo: Fran's great-niece, but she doesn't get into as much trouble as the Katie in the books. Fran lives in New York City, three blocks from Central Park, where she can often be found bird-watching and daydreaming. She writes at her dining room table, without the help of her naughty cats, Goldy and Chaim.

About the Illustrator

Tammie Lyon, the illustrator of the Katie Woo and Pedro series, says that these characters are two of her favorites. Tammie has illustrated work for Disney, Scholastic, Simon and Schuster, Penguin, HarperCollins, and Amazon Publishing, to name a few. She is also an author/illustrator of her own stories. Her first picture book, *Olive and Snowflake*, was released to starred reviews from *Kirkus* and *School Library Journal*. Tammie lives in Cincinnati, Ohio, with her husband Lee and two dogs, Amos and Artie. She spends her days working in her home studio in the woods, surrounded by wildlife and, of course, two mostly-always-sleeping dogs.

Glossary

clue (KLOO)—something that helps someone find something or solve a mystery

feather (FETH-er)—one of the many soft, light things that cover a bird's body

mystery (MISS-tur-ee)—a puzzle or crime that needs to be solved

noisy (NOI-zee)—making a lot of loud sounds

squirrel (SKWIR-uhl)—a small animal with a bushy tail

tracks (TRAKS)—marks left behind by a person or animal

All About Mysteries

A mystery is a story where the main characters must figure out a puzzle or solve a crime. Let's think about *The Mystery of the Snow Puppy*.

Plot

In a mystery, the plot focuses on solving a problem. What is the problem in this story?

Clues

To solve a mystery, readers should look for clues. What are some of the clues in this mystery?

Red Herrings

Red herrings are bad clues. They do not help solve the mystery. Sometimes they even make the mystery harder to solve. What clues in this story were red herrings?

Thinking About the Story

1. What ideas did Katie and Pedro use to find Koko? Make a list. Circle the idea that worked the best.

2. What would you do if your pet ran away? Write a paragraph.

3. Look back at the pictures. How do you think Katie felt when Koko was missing? What clues tell you this?

Investigating Animal Tracks

Some of Katie and Pedro's clues in this story were animal tracks. This is a fun way to investigate animal tracks outside. Be sure to ask a grown-up for permission!

Make an Animal Track Plot

What you need:

- mesh splatter screen (you will use this as a sifter)

- bucket

- shovel

What you do:

1. Clear about one square yard of soil so it is free of grass, sticks, and leaves. You are trying to get to the soil underneath.

2. Dig up some dirt and put it in the bucket. Be sure to keep the soil level as you dig.

3. Put the dirt on the screen. Sift it onto the cleared area. You want to spread a layer of dust all over the cleared area.

4. Test your plot by carefully placing your hand on the plot. Lift your hand and notice your handprint. Sift the dirt over your print so the plot is ready for animals.

5. Check your plot every morning. Did any animals visit over night? What kind of animals have stopped by?

Solve more mysteries with Katie and Pedro!

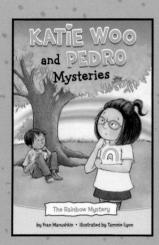

KATIE WOO
and PEDRO
Mysteries

The Rainbow Mystery

by Fran Manushkin • illustrated by Tammie Lyon

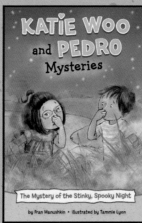

KATIE WOO
and PEDRO
Mysteries

The Mystery of the Stinky, Spooky Night

by Fran Manushkin • illustrated by Tammie Lyon

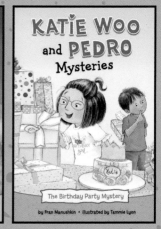

KATIE WOO
and PEDRO
Mysteries

The Birthday Party Mystery

by Fran Manushkin • illustrated by Tammie Lyon